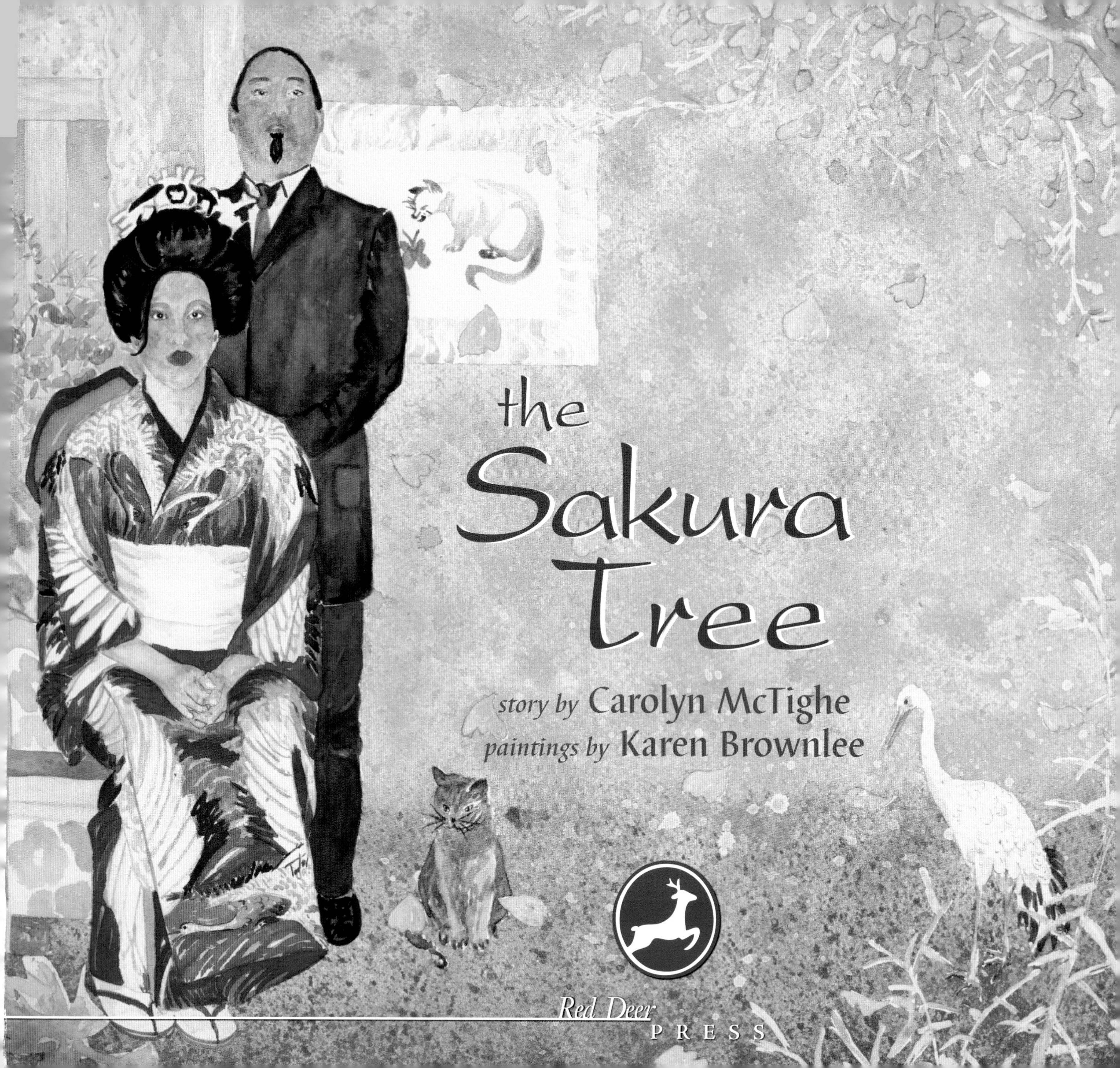

# the Sakura Tree

story by Carolyn McTighe

paintings by Karen Brownlee

Red Deer PRESS

Once there lived three Japanese sisters. The eldest sister's name was Aki, which means autumn. She was named this because she was as graceful as the gold and red leaves that swirl gently to earth in the autumn breeze. The middle sister's name was Fuyu, which means winter. She was named this because her skin was as fair as the whitest winter's snow. The youngest sister's name was Haruko, which means spring. She was named this because her silky black hair smelled of the sweetest spring blossoms.

The three sisters loved their home in Sendai, which was nestled beneath green hillsides and majestic purple mountains. During the warm summer, the sisters explored the Banji cliffs and played in the waters of the Hirose-gawa River. They loved to watch the waves of the Pacific Ocean rolling to shore and look skyward to the snow monsters on Mt. Zao. The sisters could not imagine living anywhere other than their lovely city of trees.

One day their father told them that they would be taking a long trip from their beloved home to a place called Canada, far across the ocean. "I love you very much, but we are a poor family," their father told them. "In Sendai, I cannot give you the life you deserve, so I must send you away to find happiness in a new land. Waiting for you in Canada will be three men to whom you have been promised. They are kind men who will marry you and give you a good life." Their father explained that their new husbands had chosen them as brides from their pictures.

Though the sisters were unhappy to leave their family and their homeland, they obeyed their father and readied themselves for the long journey. Before leaving, each sister decided to take one thing with that would remind her of her family and her home.

"I will bring my beautiful silk kimono," Aki said, as she was the most sensible. "I will wear it on my wedding day, and its bright colors will remind me of our family's love."

"I will bring my red violin," said Fuyu, as she was the most sentimental. "On nights when I long to be home, I will play it, and in my mind I will hear the sound of Sendai's spring winds rustling the leaves of the zelkova trees."

"I will bring three sakura tree seeds," Haruko said, as she was the most whimsical. "When I arrive at my new home, I will plant the seeds and three beautiful cherry trees will grow. Each spring, when they bloom, I will smell their sweet perfume and be reminded of my two gentle sisters and our home far away."

Once the three sisters had gathered their meager belongings, they boarded the huge steamship that would take them to their new home in Canada.

As they traveled across the ocean, Aki gently ran her hands across her beautiful silk kimono. She dreamed of her future husband and wondered what her life would be like in her new home. Fuyu played her red violin and sang songs she had learned back in Sendai. Haruko unfolded her white silk scarf and looked at the tiny sakura tree seeds that nestled in the fabric's soft folds. She dreamed of the trees' beautiful pink blossoms, while Fuyu played her violin and sang the "Cherry Blossom" song.

| | |
|---|---|
| *Sakura sakura* | Cherry blossoms, cherry blossoms, |
| *Yayoi no sora wa* | Across the April skies, |
| *Miwatasu kagiri* | As far as you can see. |
| *Kasumi ka kumo ka* | They look like a mist or clouds, |
| *Nioi zo izuru* | Blooming fragrantly. |
| *Izaya izaya* | Let's go! Let's go! |
| *Mini yu kan* | Let's go see them! |

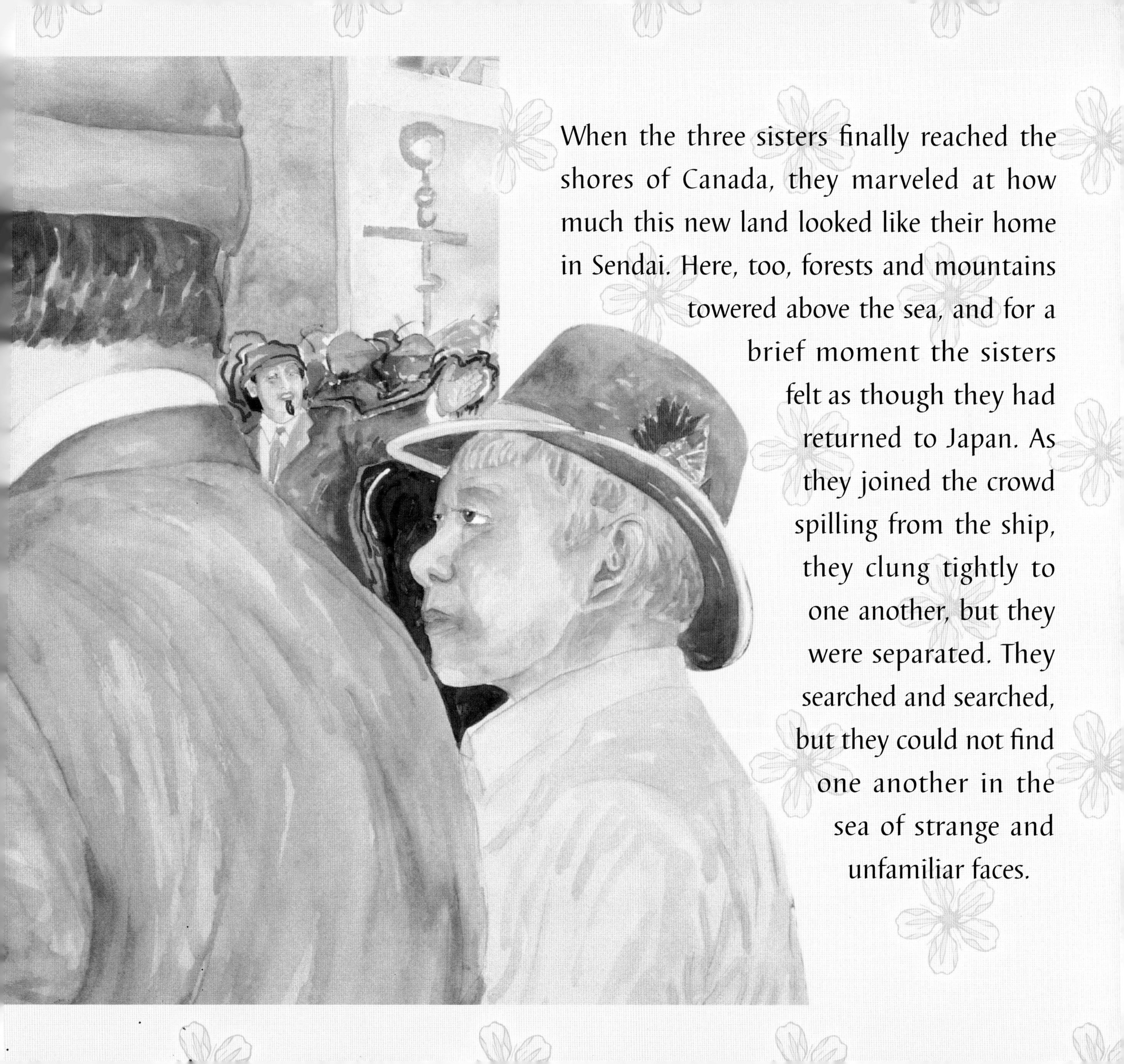

When the three sisters finally reached the shores of Canada, they marveled at how much this new land looked like their home in Sendai. Here, too, forests and mountains towered above the sea, and for a brief moment the sisters felt as though they had returned to Japan. As they joined the crowd spilling from the ship, they clung tightly to one another, but they were separated. They searched and searched, but they could not find one another in the sea of strange and unfamiliar faces.

Aki began to wander through the crowd and was eventually greeted by a tall man named Yukio. "I am a farmer, and I live in a town called Delta," Yukio said. "Your father sent me your picture, and you are going to become my wife."

Fuyu was also lost among the crowd and was searching for her sisters when she met Jiro. "I am a fisherman, and I live in a town called Steveston," Jiro said. "I recognize you from your photograph. Soon we will be married, and I will become your husband."

Beans
Beans

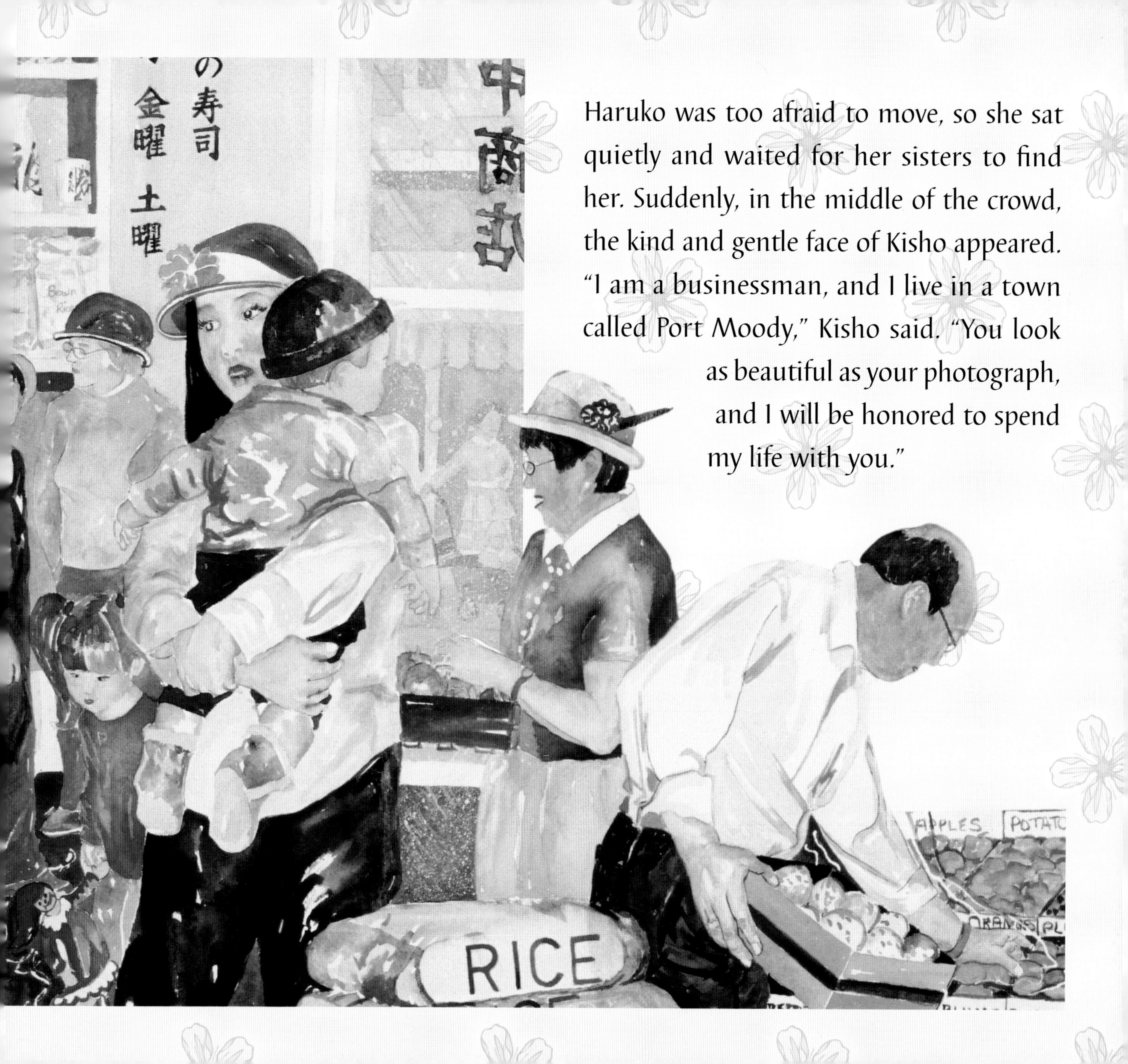


Haruko was too afraid to move, so she sat quietly and waited for her sisters to find her. Suddenly, in the middle of the crowd, the kind and gentle face of Kisho appeared. "I am a businessman, and I live in a town called Port Moody," Kisho said. "You look as beautiful as your photograph, and I will be honored to spend my life with you."

Aki, Fuyu and Haruko found happiness in their new homes with their new husbands, but they missed each other very much. Over the years, Aki often brought out the beautiful silk kimono she wore on her wedding day. As she looked at herself in the mirror, she remembered her two younger sisters, and her heart was sad. She longed to see Sendai and her family again, but then she saw Yukio's smiling face, and her sadness ended.

Fuyu became mother to a lovely little girl, and every night as she put her daughter to bed, she would play her a song on her red violin. Her daughter's favorite was the "Cherry Blossom" song. Sometimes playing the song would make Fuyu weep as she remembered playing and singing it to her two sisters, but when she looked into her daughter's eyes, her heart found comfort and her sadness ceased.

When Haruko arrived at her new home, the first thing she did was plant the seeds she had brought all the way from Japan. She tenderly cared for the young trees year after year until one spring they began to blossom. Though there were many trees in her neighborhood, there were none as beautiful and fragrant as Haruko's sakura trees when their branches hung heavy with clusters of pink flowers.

One day a strong wind began to blow, and the tiny pink blossoms were gently picked from their boughs and carried high into the air. They swirled and soared across the countryside like a springtime snowfall. A handful of blossoms landed on the doorsteps of Aki and Fuyu. They recognized the delicate shape and fragrant perfume of the sakura petals and were reminded of the tiny seeds their little sister had brought to Canada from Japan.

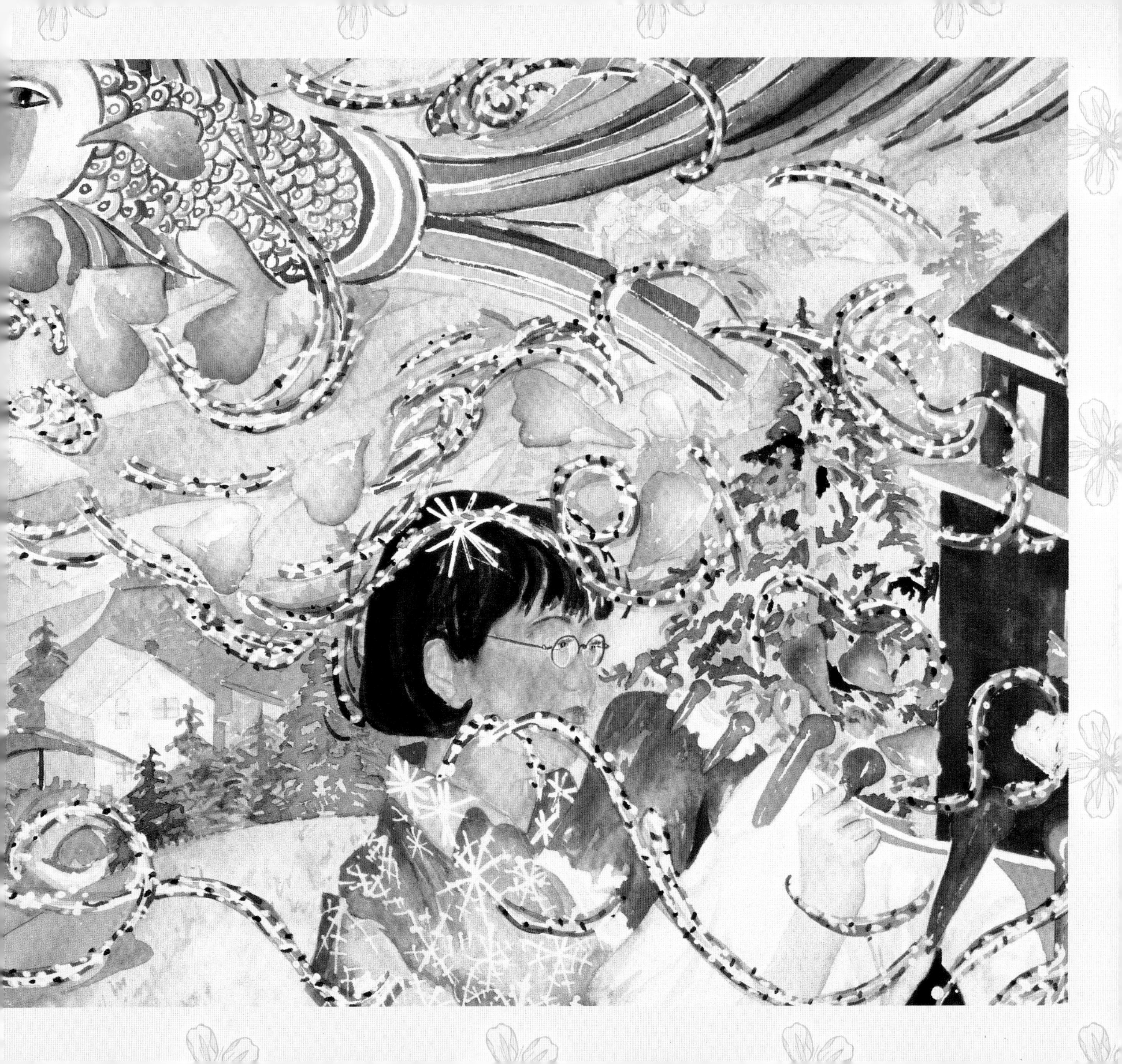

Aki and Fuyu each decided to follow the trail of pink petals, hoping their paths would lead to Haruko. Every fragrant step carried the sisters closer and closer to each other. Far from their homes, they began to grow weary, but then their paths finally met.

"I can hardly believe you are here!" Aki cried. "I have missed you so much and have dreamed of the day when we would be together again."

"I too have dreamed of that day, and through the years I never forgot about you and Haruko," Fuyu confessed.

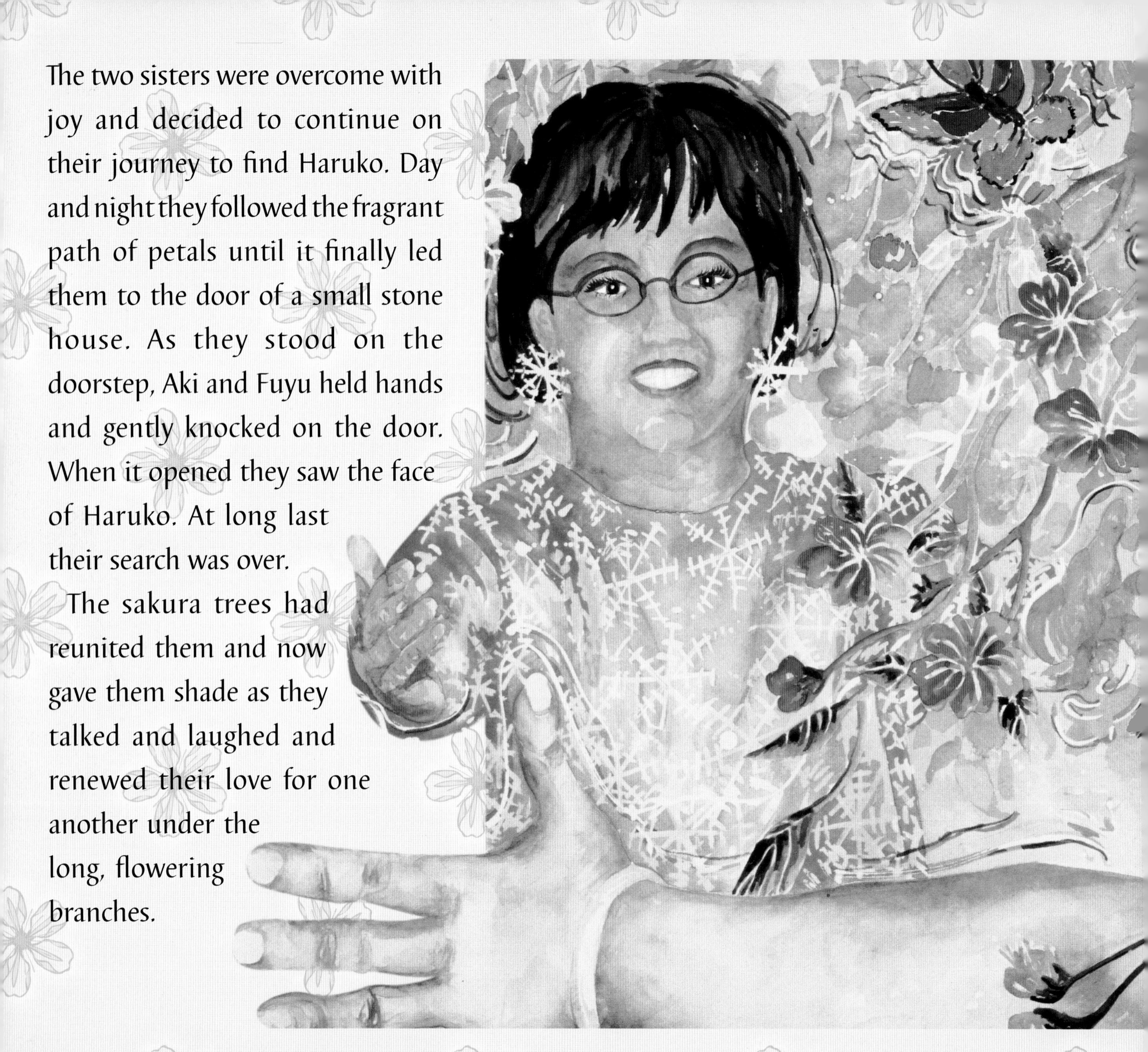

The two sisters were overcome with joy and decided to continue on their journey to find Haruko. Day and night they followed the fragrant path of petals until it finally led them to the door of a small stone house. As they stood on the doorstep, Aki and Fuyu held hands and gently knocked on the door. When it opened they saw the face of Haruko. At long last their search was over.

The sakura trees had reunited them and now gave them shade as they talked and laughed and renewed their love for one another under the long, flowering branches.

Though they still lived many miles apart, every spring when the sakura trees bloomed and their blossoms sailed high into the air on the spring wind, the sisters would come together and remember their life in Sendai.

Published in the United States in 2008

5 4 3 2 1



Northern Lights Books for Children are published by
Red Deer Press
A Fitzhenry & Whiteside Company
1512, 1800 – 4 Street SW Calgary AB T2S 2S5
www.reddeerpress.com
www.fitzhenry.ca

Credits
Edited for the Press by Peter Carver
Cover design by Naoko Masuda
Text design by Boldface Technologies
Printed and bound in China by Paramount Book Art for Red Deer Press

Acknowledgements
Red Deer Press acknowledges the support of the Canada Council for the Arts, which last year invested $20.1 million in writing and publishing throughout Canada. Financial support also provided by Government of Canada through the Book Publishing Industry Development Program (BPIDP).

Canada Council for the Arts  Conseil des Arts du Canada  Canada

Library and Archives Canada Cataloguing in Publication
McTighe, Carolyn
The sakura tree / story by Carolyn McTighe ; paintings by Karen Brownlee.
ISBN 978-0-88995-354-3
I. Brownlee, Karen II. Title.
PS8625.T55S36 2007 jC813'.6 C2007-900167-X

Red Deer
PRESS

For my father for inspiring in me a love of all things literary.

–Carolyn McTighe

For Ray, Robyn and Logan Brownlee, and for my Japanese-Canadian models, cultural consultants and dear friends, many of whom are descendants of picture brides. *Jinji o tsukushite tenmei o matsu.* (Do your best and wait for God's decision.)

–Karen Brownlee

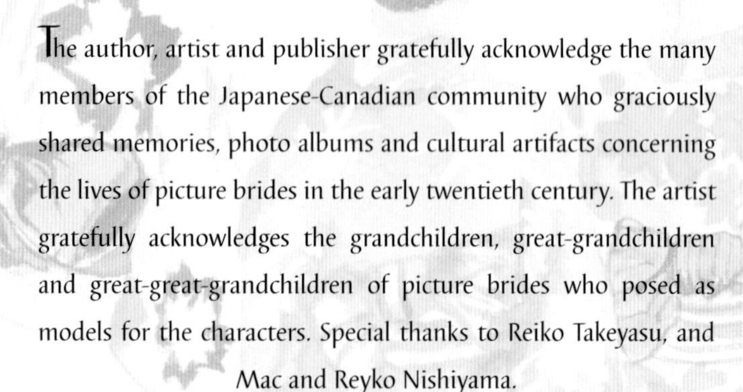

The author, artist and publisher gratefully acknowledge the many members of the Japanese-Canadian community who graciously shared memories, photo albums and cultural artifacts concerning the lives of picture brides in the early twentieth century. The artist gratefully acknowledges the grandchildren, great-grandchildren and great-great-grandchildren of picture brides who posed as models for the characters. Special thanks to Reiko Takeyasu, and Mac and Reyko Nishiyama.

The artist and publisher gratefully acknowledge the support of the Edmonton Japanese Community Association; the Calgary Japanese Community Association; the Nikka Yuko Centennial Garden, Lethbridge, Alberta; Tollestrup Construction Ltd.; Ashley Zeller; Susan, Sydney, Cameron and Neo Takeda; Dr. and Mrs. Roland and Brenda Ikuta and family; Harold and Doreen Lissel; Sylvia Oishi and Terry Hanna family; Dr. Wes Fournier; Shirley Kopitzke; and Jan Foster.